Gods of Legend

ODIN

ERIC BRAUN

WORLD BOOK

BOLT

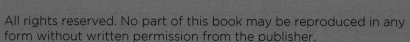

This World Book edition of *Odin*
is published by agreement between
Black Rabbit Books and World Book, Inc.
© 2018 Black Rabbit Books,
2140 Howard Dr. West,
North Mankato, MN 56003 U.S.A.
World Book, Inc.,
180 North LaSalle St., Suite 900,
Chicago, IL 60601 U.S.A.

Marysa Storm, editor; Michael Sellner, designer; Omay Ayres,
photo researcher

Library of Congress Control Number: 2016049943

ISBN: 978-0-7166-9312-3

Printed in the United States at CG Book Printers,
North Mankato, Minnesota, 56003. 3/17

Image Credits
Alamy: AF archive, 28;
Aloysius Patrimonio, 21; Ivy Close
Images, 16–17, 18; Commons.wikime-
dia.org: Lorenz Frølich / Haukurth, 6 (top);
Sokol_92, 6 (bottom); iStock: berdsigns, 10;
duncan1890, 12, 26–27; vukkostic, 4–5; The
Johnson Galleries: Howard David Johnson, 19, 20
(top), 23, 23–24; Shutterstock: Kaukin Andrey, 31;
Molodec, 1; Rafinaded, 3; Vuk Kostic, 9, 32, Back
Cover; Willierossin, 20 (bottom); www.johndote-
gowski.com: John Dotegowski, Cover, 15
Every effort has been made to contact copy-
right holders for material reproduced
in this book. Any omissions will be
rectified in subsequent printings
if notice is given to the
publisher.

CONTENTS

CHAPTER 1

An ANCIENT Story

At the beginning of time, an evil giant ruled the **universe**. His name was Ymir. Other giants and the first gods came from him. Odin was one of those gods. Odin and his brothers did not like the giants. They fought with Ymir and killed him. Odin then became ruler of the universe.

Some stories say that
before anything else,
there was only fire and ice.
The fire melted the ice.
From the melted ice came
Ymir and a cow. All living
things came from them.

Making the Earth

Odin and his brothers used Ymir's **flesh** to make the earth. They made mountains from his bones. His blood became oceans and lakes. They raised up his skull. The sky came from it.

One day, Odin and his brothers walked along a beach. They saw two fallen trees. Odin lifted the trees. He breathed life into them. The trees turned into the first humans.

CHAPTER 2

The Norse

The story of Ymir and Odin is a Norse **myth**. **Ancient** people told stories to explain the world. Many myths were about gods. Norse people believed gods lived among them.

Norse people lived in northern Europe from the 700s to about 1100. Vikings were Norse warriors.

THE WORLD OF THE ANCIENT NORSE

Vikings came from what is now **Norway**, **Sweden**, and Denmark. They spread their beliefs to other places.

GREENLAND

ICELAND

IRELAND

UNITED
KINGDOM

RUSSIA

GERMANY

FRANCE

A Powerful God

Odin is one of the oldest Norse gods. He is also one of the most important. Odin was the father of all gods and people. Odin was powerful too. But he was not all-knowing. Stories say Odin always tried to gain more knowledge.

Odin was called "Allfather."

Appearance

Myths say Odin was scary to look at. He had only one eye. Stories say he traded his other eye for **wisdom**. Myths also say he wore a big hat when traveling. He carried a large spear too. It never missed its target.

PET RAVENS

SPOKE IN POETRY

MISSING EYE

ODIN ALLFATHER

PET WOLVES

CHAPTER 3

FAMILY
and Animals

Stories said Odin's wife was Frigg. She could see the future. Odin and Frigg had a son. They named him Balder. He was gentle and kind.

Odin was also known as Woden. The day Wednesday is named after him. Wednesday means "Woden's Day."

SLEIPNIR

GRAY COAT

EIGHT LEGS

TRAVELS OVER SEA AND SKY

The Best Horse

Odin lived with many animals. One of them was his horse, Sleipnir. Sleipnir had eight legs. It ran faster than any other horse. It could travel over the sea and in the sky.

Ravens and Wolves

Two ravens sat on Odin's shoulders. One was called Hugin. The other was named Munin. Their names meant "thought" and "memory." The birds flew all over looking for knowledge. They brought back what they found to Odin.

Odin also had two wolves. He gave them food from his table. Odin did not need to eat.

YGGDRASIL

The Norse believed the **universe** had three levels. The levels were part of a giant tree. The tree was called Yggdrasil (IG-druh-sil).

MIDDLE LEVEL
where humans and giants live

TOP LEVEL
where the gods live

RAINBOW BRIDGE
connects top level to middle level

LOWER LEVEL
the underworld

25

CHAPTER 4

Gods and BATTLES

Norse gods were not perfect. Stories say they fought with giants and each other. Unlike Greek or Roman gods, Norse gods could die.

One myth tells of a huge battle in the future. The fight is between the gods and giants. In it, all the gods and giants will die. Stories say the **monstrous** wolf Fenrir will kill Odin.

The battle is called Ragnarök.

Odin Today

Many Norse myths have been forgotten. But some were written down. Many years ago, people discovered ancient poems in Iceland. The poems told Norse stories. That is one of the ways people know about Odin today.

Now, many movies, books, and games feature Norse gods. The characters were created hundreds of years ago. But they live on today.

ancient (AYN-shunt)—from a time long ago

flesh (FLESH)—the soft parts of the body of an animal or person

monstrous (MON-struhs)—very ugly, cruel, or vicious

myth (MITH)—a story told to explain a practice, belief, or natural occurrence

raven (REY-vuhn)—a large bird with black feathers

universe (YOO-nuh-vurs)—all of space and everything in it

wisdom (WIZ-duhm)—the natural ability to understand things that most other people cannot understand

BOOKS

Napoli, Donna Jo. *Treasury of Norse Mythology: Stories of Intrigue, Trickery, Love, and Revenge.* Washington, D.C.: National Geographic, 2015.

Shecter, Vicky Alvear. *Thor Speaks!: A Guide to the Viking Realms by the Nordic God of Thunder.* Secrets of the Ancient Gods. Honesdale, PA: Boyds Mills Press, 2015.

Thompson, Ben. *Guts & Glory: The Vikings.* New York: Little, Brown and Company, 2015.

WEBSITES

Middle Ages: Vikings
www.ducksters.com/history/middle_ages_vikings.php

Ten Facts about the Vikings
www.ngkids.co.uk/history/10-facts-about-the-vikings

Vikings: Beliefs and Stories
www.bbc.co.uk/schools/primaryhistory/vikings/beliefs_and_stories/

INDEX